Aunt Sur

I'm aware + and distant, and I hope you understand this is not a reflection of my love for you. We have more in common you and I. I believe my ability to write and create "art" is not a skill one learns like carpentry or ballet, but is something deeper. Something knit together in ones DNA. So, I want to thank you for this gift because I am 100% certain my ability to write poems and stories is a gift from you.

I Love you and will always be with you, no matter how far away I might be...

♡

Chris

RA PRESS
100 Kennedy Drive #53
South Burlington, VT. 05403

copyright 2012
Christopher Ricker
all rights reserved
ISBN 978-1-4675-0123-1

LUNCH AT NOONMARK

A Collection of Short Stories
& Poems
by Christopher Ricker

Dedicated to:
Jim Moore

Special Thanks to:
Heather M. and
Douglas & Sandra Ricker

"Use what language you will, you can never say anything but what you are"
    Ralph Waldo Emerson

Fireberry Acre

'Klee Klee Klee,' called a kestrel, playing coy
from an island of resurrected pine.

I crossed her fire clear acre where knotted
blueberry bushels carpeted a once dead
and tawny ground.

Feeling something like a flea bite at my ankle, I
looked to see a cloud of hungry black flies hang
above my boot lace.

Their gnawing swelled into small volcanoes
erupting a freckle-speck of blood that ran dirty
down my leg and onto my woolen sock.

Needless to say they had gotten
the better of me.

It's hard not to note those big telephone wires
floating between skinned tree corpses, fenced up
against those dangerous automobiles.

Icicles

Last night's frost
has bearded my car
with fuzzy icicles.
      At the feeder
the Goldie's are being
    unreasonable.
Lately, we've noticed
that no neighborhood
children have
made snowmen.
   The only enjoyable
constant has been an
     ornery house cat.

We think the sheriff's
* department might be*
*   on its case.*

Everyone's patiently
  anticipating the sweet
   smell of
     sugar house.

Just Beyond the Hill

"Show me a hero, and I'll write you a tragedy."
F. Scott Fitzgerald

Everything was the color of wheat now. What was once grass and shrubs and green knolls with white capes had changed. Moisture gathered in the air with a ceramic sky ready to crack under the pressure of December. It was a strange month, one of the warmest beginnings to a northern winter on record.

I rounded the truck off of the main road. Tarmac gave way to dirt and gravel. The back road curved over exposed culverts. The white well-kept homes gave way to chipped brown cabins, slovenly ranch style shacks and debilitated trailers. The prolix light darkened under a canopy of evergreens and competing hardwoods. Looser and looser the substrate became as the truck climbed one of the steeper hills. Dropping into a lower gear the engine growled at first, the gears caught and the climb resumed.

After a twenty minute trek on this dilapidated back road, I arrived at the site on Sugar House Road, an address you wouldn't find on any *New York State Road Atlas*, though this section of the Adirondacks has been settled since pre-Revolutionary War times. My directions were all intuitive now. I would never be able to point it out on a map, nor could I even explain where it was with any exactitude.

Pulling into the drive, the first thing noticeable in the yard was an endless supply of rust. Cars, tractors, presses, scrap metal parts, an engine hanging from shackles in a gnarly wolf tree. Blocking the drive from continuing to the backyard was a mountain of metal. Iron, steel, stainless steel, brass, copper, aluminum, zinc, and nickel that took the form of everything from water pipes to fencing - all parts that had once been extracted from the earth to now just junk-settled surface odds and ends.

When I exited the truck, I heard from an unknown distance a pack of Roland's mangy dogs approach. The howling would have been terrifying to any unwanted visitor who might also have been put off by the bullet-speckled "No Trespassing" signs scattered about the yard.

From a corner of the house an assortment of the wreckyard dogs came charging, of varying shapes and sizes, resembling one another only by their dirty-mutt coats and bloodthirsty sounding yowls.

"Hey boys," I yelled over their barks as they approached.

When they reached me the first two hounds attempted to jump me. I pushed back. A small rat of a dog began grabbing at my pant leg with her teeth. She tugged and tugged, throwing her head back and forth. When she made an effort to readjust her grip I gave the bitch a little kick. This startled her enough so that, when she refocused, she spent her energy attacking one of the other hounds.

Walking onto the slanted porch of the ranch I knocked at the screen door and shouted into the living room, "Roland? Hey, Roland! It's Topher. Are you in there?"

A torn screen allowed me to see inside to the living room of the home. The hardwood floor had an ash color. There was a big plaid lazy-boy chair with matching couch that had one of its cushions missing. In its place a wooden desk chair resided. When I made to head off the porch, I noticed a five gallon bucket full of empty Pabst Blue Ribbon cans.

I descended the rickety steps and traversed mounds of junk. Halfway around the house I shouted for Roland again. There was a small root vegetable garden by the side of his home. Bowling-ball sized turnips and rutabagas protruded from the ground wearing leafy green crowns. It was odd for the earth not to be frozen this time of year. Because of this peculiar warm weather, the growing season had been extended a good bit. The change seemed a useful benefit for Roland though I think the garden had not been harvested due to laziness rather than to plan.

"Where the hell is this son-of-a…?"

Near the back of the house I heard clanking. The sound reminded me of an auto shop - a noise I had heard as a kid when my Dad had attempted to play mechanic in our front yard at home.

"Shit! Shit! … Fuck this goddamn piece of shit! God, that smarts!" the voice being followed by a sound that could only be described as the impact of a wrench bouncing off a car hood. This excited the dogs and they took to running ahead of me, making a beeline bend around the back corner of the house.

As I followed them I saw Roland cursing and kicking at everything in sight, including the little ankle-biting dog. *(Roland, my nickname for Matt, north country knight errant devoted to lost causes.)*

I leaned against the house to watch his performance. It was quite entertaining. Ever since we had met in college, Roland and I had always enjoyed watching one another squirm a little. It was a brotherly love. We were both competitive and yet supportive of each another. It seemed like yesterday when first we had met. It had been almost six years since we had sparked a friendship as students. It was in the basement classroom of the Griswold Library at Green Mountain College in Vermont.

For some strategically strange educational purpose, Professor Hopple, in one of his lessons on Public Policy, had instigated a battle of physical strength between Roland and me in his classroom. I'm sure the Professor thought it would be cleverly experimental. The result was outrageous. Roland and I knew little about one another, but could instantly see the fire in the other's eyes as we were positioned to wrestle in front of our classmates. Hopple shouted *Go*, and before anyone could blink an eye, Roland and I were grappling. The whole ordeal was over in less than a minute. Our physical prowess was equally matched. We tossed one another across the floor an even number of times and, before things could escalate to an uncontrollable degree, time was called. The fight had ended. I don't think Professor Hopple expected such an outcome, nor the animal emergence that occurred in each of us. We were never again asked to participate in such a physical display during class, although there would be several occasions outside the classroom during that semester where the match would resurrect itself.

It was the evening after this bizarre Public Policy class that Roland and I first realized our brotherhood. It was over the bottle of gin that we drank out of mason jars. We sang songs. We talked into the early morning hours.

I now began a slow-clap of mock applause as Roland's tantrum subsided. He turned quickly with that same fire I had seen six years earlier. His eyes changed quickly when he noticed me leaning against the house laughing.

"Bastard. Where the hell did you come from?"

"I thought I'd stop in. I haven't seen you in forever. Julia is away with her mother for a week and I didn't want to spend all my time alone up in Burlington. You know the way my mind gets when no one's around. At first I love the empty quiet, but then those wheels start turning and everything gets all gloomy. You know what I'm saying?"

"Yeah, I do. You know what it's been like since Marilyn left me. That's why I have the dogs, Topher. When I get really lonely I just head into the bar. I know the constable well, so he no longer checks me if he notices my truck in town at night. And even if he were to take me to the tank, I'd at least have some company for the night. Y'know what I'm saying?"

Roland looked about, picked up a rag and cleaned some grease off of his thick hands. "Hey, brotha, it's great to see you."

We hugged, padding one another on the back. It was good to see him.

The dogs started up their deafening commotion that not only consisted of barking and howling, but also of running in a whirlpool motion that was dizzying to watch.

"Shut up!" howled Roland. And in the role of an alpha dog, everything became silent.

"Fuck, let's go inside and have a drink. I bet you're hungry after that ride. We can make some venison steaks and eggs. A man-meal. You know what I'm saying?"

"A man meal, huh?"

"Don't be cheeky, you son-of-a…"

Roland led me up the back porch stairs. I looked around at the peeling gray paint of the screened-in porch interior. More tools and a bench stood in one corner. To the other side was a Honey Bee Harvesting station. Roland was living many lives. Hermit. Mechanic. Writer. Saint. Drunk. He was militant and sensitive all at one time. Roland's wit could be venomous, but his compassion and loyalty to those he loved was unconditional.

It was only once early on in our friendship that Roland and I had really gotten into a nasty confrontation. Words flew like daggers. It ended with us not speaking for nearly a week. On the eighth day, after having artfully avoided each other on campus in the interim, Roland and I finally approached one another. Coming to a stop a few feet apart, we looked hard at one another, eyeball to eyeball, so to speak.

It was Roland who initiated the conversation.

"I don't really remember what we were fighting about."

"I don't either. I think it was something about you being a bastard," I said.

"I know. We are both big pricks, but I want to get over this. It's pretty silly. So maybe we can forget it. It's not like we can go the rest of our lives not talking. Ya know what I mean?"

And just like that our quarrel was squashed.

We sat across from one another wearing stupid smirks at the kitchen table under a yellow fanlight. The first beer went down with the conversation revolving about what each of us had been up to in recent months.

With our second beer the conversation started to pick up some steam. It had always been that way between us. We brought the best and worst out in one another. We were the type of men who kept our cards close to the vest. That might be why it was always the third or fourth beer that got the conversation truly started.

"So, when are you going to get out of this dump and move up to Burlington?" I asked.

"Well, you know, I have this house and all these dogs. It's like stocks and bonds. I can't just pick up and leave."

"Yes, you can, Dude. Listen, Mar is gone. She's not coming back. If you think staying here and letting the ground and trees reclaim you is the way to go, you're an idiot."

"Don't you think I know that? It's just the bills and…"

"Don't talk to me about debt. That's all I have. That's all everyone in our generation has. Like our parents, we are prone to debt. That's how we learned to get into these situations."

"We can't blame our parents for everything," Roland rebutted.

"I'm not saying that. It's just... It's just that we're living in a world our parents knew nothing about. They never saw this one comin'. They made us ill-prepared to deal with the trials of *the future*. Same with their parents before them. How can people prepare their children for the future when they have no idea what's to come?" I slugged my beer. "I'm sorry, Roland. I'm still bitter about this student loan debt, even after all this time."

"Well, you're preaching to the choir, brotha!" Roland replied. "Let's change the subject. This is all god-awful stuff."

I reached into the old 1970's ice box and pulled out two more cold beers. Roland looked up.

"Topher, put those away. I have something much better."

Roland stood and walked through the corridor and opened a door. I saw him disappear down cellar steps. Banging and crashing went on for a while before I heard his return up those same stairs a short time later.

Sliding through the door, smoothly landing in his chair beside me, Roland placed a large clear bottle on the table. It was a growler. Inside was clear liquor. In my head I was hoping it wasn't vodka. I always had had trouble getting vodka down the pipe. Anything else works for me, but when it comes to vodka...

"*Hudson Corn Whiskey*. Some really good stuff," Roland promised.

He placed two glasses down on a makeshift tray (in reality an apple crate) and poured the glasses half full. I smelled, toasted my friend and took a good mouthful. It was warm and smooth, not harsh nor scratchy, the way some bad whiskeys ride down the throat.

"This is some good stuff," I said, smiling in approval.

A few whiskeys later, Roland pulled out his new shotgun from under a pile of discarded awnings. It was a great piece of shiny smooth hardware. The muzzle, pump, and stock were midnight black.

"It's a police model Mossberg 12 gauge," said Roland.

I held the gun. It was cold. I pumped the action and felt its cool transition. There are many guns in the world, each with their own purpose. Purpose defines each weapon. When holding long barrel shotguns, you can imagine being on a pond, seeing the blue sky changing its color, turning to purple with veins of pink rolling the dusk, the shadow of the cat tails making the heavens seem on fire. That's when you see the geese. That's when you pull the shotgun to the sky and line that bead on the mallard and...

But this gun gave you a sense of belligerence. Its main purpose was to kill. To kill a human and not from a distance, like a rifle for a deer, but close-up. The snub nose made it an inaccurate shot. To take someone out with this gun you had to be close enough to see the person's eyes.

"It's my new home defense," Roland grinned.

We were both feeling the whiskey now, but I

was not yet drunk. I knew that my time here was short; that soon I would need to be back on the road. I regretted the squandered moments from our past, and the moments, like now, also misspent. But that's the game. Roland knew it. I knew it.

"One more?" Roland asked already knowing my answer.

"I'd love to, but..."

"Eh! I get it. Don't make excuses." Roland understood better than anyone. How we had been together almost every day for years, neither of us understanding the dark that would one day come to fill our lives. We had lived those great wild years of youth together, being naive to both the thought and the concepts of age, marriage, divorce, and debt. Many nights we had spent late, talking about living in the moment, not knowing that the moments pass faster than the seasons, that the only thing we belonged to was the fragility of the years passing, with death at the goal line.

I had watched Roland's life change. I had been there with him through the death of his father, mother, brother, even favorite dog. Over the years I had met the women who had come and gone in his life. None of them could be blamed for leaving him; nor did he himself blame them for leaving him. It was all just time passing to him.

"Well, Happy Birthday, Brotha," I said to him.

"Happy Birthday, Topher."

Before Roland, I had never met anyone whose birthday I shared. Nor have I since. It was just one of those things, one of the many oddities in this all too blue a world.

I gave Roland a final hug before I jumped into the truck. Backing out of the drive I watched Roland and his house recede before me. He had his gun resting over his shoulder like some sideburn outlaw. The dogs howled and jumped and rolled and did what dogs do in yards.

I was a hundred yards down the road when I heard the gun go off. The shot rumbled through the trees. I slammed on the brakes. A chill ran up my back like the devil himself licking spine. Dark thoughts ran through my head. My heart raced.

As I was about to turn the truck around I heard the shots continue.

Six shots rang out through the pines.

I knew then that the gun was empty. Starting the truck and placing it into first gear, I began my drive back home.

Splitting

My double bit
shines like a sparkler
    in the trees.
Its hickory
handle warped from years
    of hewing timber.
Many nostalgic days it must
have spent in outbuildings.
Dreaming of deer
camps, and the days before.
Plenty of its time
now has been used up
    chipping away at
weathering wood piles.

Adirondack Americana

If I had stumbled across Valkyrie
    meeting at the water's edge
I would not have been astonished.
It was half expected
in a backdrop of dock lights, shining
in the dampened unoccupied
dark dwelling in the midst of
    corrupt fireflies.
Distant hills rupture the cobalt mood
    of paradise, with craggy incisors
escaping the margins of an underworld.
Parading a string-band symphony
on the bandstand that aligns brown-stone
alleys and moody jetties in the village.
It was a lustful avalanche
    that struck the last star
reigning over the women's small cribs
    and little sleeping lives.

Journey to Indian Lake

"It's one of nature's ways that we often feel closer to distant generations than to the generation immediately preceding us."
     Igor Stravinsky

The blue Lincoln sputtered. The journey had begun. Only 267 miles and most of it highway driving. Papa hummed *Sinatra* songs while lightly guiding the steering wheel. I was much smaller then and could barely see over the front seat, yet the steering wheel was in plain sight. *(I do wonder now if steering wheels have shrunk over the last few decades of car design.)*

Grandpa looked like a Ship's Captain, drifting the car in the wake of tractor trailers bound for exotic ports of call like Vermont, New Hampshire, Maine, and even places Canadian - places I knew nothing about, being a little tyke from New York City.

Now and then, Nana would turn around and smile at me from behind large-rimmed glasses. Her blue hair never stirred in the rambling air that seemed desperate to make its way in through the small opening in the passenger side window.

"Topher, are you excited about our weekend get-away?" Nana asked.

"Yes, Nana."

I leaned forward, making it possible to turn around in my seatbelt and look out of the rear window. Rows and rows of cars glided behind us or passed alongside in other lanes. But slowly everything urban was beginning to transform into mountain and sky as my home city, its buildings and its bridges, were becoming black specs in the distance.

At noon Nana leaned over to Papa. "George, what do you think about stopping for lunch?"

Nana always asked Papa questions in a manner you just don't hear anymore. It was a command, but an order that upheld respect for the patriarchal façade. She did this for his pride. He knew it, of course, but loved her for it.

"Sure, I guess if the '*Cricket*' back there is hungry we should," he said, looking at me through the mirror.

We drove a little further on. I watched the green interstate signs pass. Some had off-color Indian names such as *Mohawk*, while others were more difficult for me to read, although I did recognize them from my social studies textbooks.

Overpasses turned into trees, then back into signs as we sputtered along.

The dirty clouds over Albany reminded me of Staten Island - the brown brick and bright graffiti ogling at the Thru-way. The nightmarish post-industrial structures and fire escapes, caped in the greening design looked like the scary street scenes from *Willy Wonka*. I closed my eyes.

But, in a short while, I opened my eyes to a sea of green pines that would continue on as our new and constant companions.

My mind was telling me that I must be a trillion miles away from home. How long had we been on the road? Would my parents recognize me now? I could feel myself aging in the car over those interminable two and a half hours in the back seat of the Lincoln.

It was just when my mind could no longer ignore food that Nana said, "Oh, look, George - Saratoga Springs! Let's stop here for a bit. We can get lunch and have a walk around the city. You know how I love the clear redbrick of Upstate. Maybe we can even stop at the tracks."

Nana kept one hand on his shoulder while again making this *so-called* request.

"Yes, that sounds great, Muriel. Remember, though, we still need a few hours of highway time before we will be up to the cabin. I want to make sure 'Cricket' gets some rest so he doesn't get cranky." He threw a big smile back in my direction.

"No, No, I won't... I won't get cranky," I said with both an objection and a promise in mind.

Turning off the exit we were in the city of Saratoga in a very short time. The brown buildings resembled Albany somewhat, but gave this place much less of a city feel. The streets were littered with smiles and young strangely-dressed twenty-something's.

"Ah, the hooligans!" exclaimed Grandpa.

The city streets were compact. Pedestrians spilled to overflow from crowded sidewalks. Little shops with silly names boarded the Plaza. Even after all these many years, I can still picture the tiny commons centered with even smaller sculptures whose abstractness made no sense to my eyes or mind. These works were black and faced the sky - odd shapes almost exploding from the metal hodge-podge.

"Things have changed in this town. I don't think these kids go to Skidmore. They remind me of the hoodlums who loiter outside of school during the day. George, remember the hoods around Port Richmond? They are the same radioactive aftermath of those acid head hippies. Damn *Generation X*," said my grandmother.

"That's the problem with youth today," mumbled Papa.

These words worried me. Was it me he was talking about? Was I among the people who didn't get it? Was I inadequate in the eyes of real men? Was I, indeed, today's youth problem?

I feared my Papa's disapproval more than anything else.

We headed to eat at *Gaffney*'s which, according to Nana, was the best eatery in Saratoga. The door opened and I walked between Papa and Nana. The hostess led us to our table. The ceilings were high and covered with tin. Neon light from the bar reflected a glow off of the flower pattern that was mesmerizing. We were seated and I ordered chocolate milk which eventually appeared in a giant glass. Before my little hands could grab it, Papa swooped in and swiped my glass.

"Do you think we can get half of this?" Papa asked the waitress.

I was angry. It was just like Papa and Nana to always treat me like a little kid. I knew if my Mother were here, she would allow me to have the whole glass. But my frustration did not erupt into a tantrum. I knew it would have no effect on Papa. He was strong and stern. Losing my temper would only prolong my attaining the chocolate milk experience.

We ate, paid the bill and walked about the town. Nana and I walked a little behind Papa. We looked into shops. At one point, I remember passing a little girl with sky blue eyes. Her nose reminded me of mine, except it wasn't as button-like. She was holding hands with someone I presumed to be her father. He wore a ponytail and had a rough-country look to him - a look similar to the roofers I'd seen working with Papa. I tried to wave my hand at her, but she seemed to ignore me.

But it was only a few seconds later that I turned about and could have sworn that she was watching me. Maybe I was mistaken.

At the tracks I was given some popcorn. The grandstands were very exciting for everyone, but I did not understand yet what was happening.

Green, the color green, was what stuck out to me. An emerald green field centered by a brown track. A horn would go off and the crowd would roar. Everyone stood. I stood too in fear of missing something.

"Nana? Who is winning? What horse is winning?" I asked.

"Hold on, Topher. It's only just started."

I still didn't understand it. Why was all this so great? I was bored. *If someone would have told me what horse was winning, maybe I would have been excited, too.*

Eventually we left the track. Nana and Papa

must have won something there because Papa was whistling and Nana was smiling even more than usual.

I have not been back to the horse races since that time in Saratoga. I don't think any of my family has either. It might be one of those activities that ended with my grandparents' passing.

Back in the car we headed for the highway. The trees grew taller and taller as I counted them. I felt the weight on my eyelids. I fought back valiantly, trying to use the long visuals of tree trunks as braces to keep my eyes open, but, like always, the call to nap prevailed and I fell into a deep sleep.

Meadow

I'm feeling vacant,
like a sucked
out grouse egg
left in the goldenrod.

If only I too had
a skeleton.

    To be
remembered in
the coming season.

Instead of clay
    clutched straw.

    ***

A pair of barn swallows
complain a little
about my clumsiness
in the meadow,

but they have bigger
    birds to fry.

Specifically that imperial crow
    coming from a distance,
    ready for a dogfight.

Indian Lake

It was impossible. The oars seemed to weigh a ton against the water which pushed back powerfully. Over and over I attempted to move the boat forward but to no avail.

"Ok, Topher! Let me have a go at it. I don't want your head to blow a gasket," Papa said as he moved to the stern to take over.

My grandfather made it look simple, propelling the boat forward by rowing both oars in unison. When he wanted to change our direction of travel, he'd simply change his strokes by moving his arms independently. The bow would turn slightly and again he would throw himself into the oars, resuming our speed.

Papa's back was to the mountains. Our momentum was quick. When I reached into the lake the surface of the water broke, leaving a small wake.

"Topher, look!" said Papa.

Shading my eyes from the bright sun I looked to the sky. As my eyes adjusted, I found myself staring in rapture at a black silhouette.

"Wow, Papa, that's a Golden Eagle. I have a bird book in the cabin. I showed Nana all the birds we might see. This is the second largest bird in North America. That's what the book says."

"Yes, Cricket. One day you'll make us all proud. Do you still want to be a Zoologist when you grow up?"

"I want to be a Zoologist, but not one that works in a Zoo. I want to be an adventurer, an explorer. You know, like Indian Jones," I said with great conviction.

"You know, Topher, there is a lot of schooling for people who want to be scientists. You will have to get really good grades in school. Your parents and Nana and I don't have a whole lot of money saved, so you are going to have to figure out a way." He then took on the look of a preacher. "And don't get involved with borrowing or taking out loans. They'll only get you in trouble."

"By that time I will be ok. You see, Papa, I love nature. I couldn't imagine not spending time working outside. Mom always says *You have to do what you love*. She tells me that one day I will grow up to be a great man. Just like you, Papa," I said smiling at him.

"That you will be, little Cricket," Papa smiled proudly.

It had been about thirty minutes since we'd left Nana on the dock playing bridge with the O'Brien's.

Reaching the rocky shore on the far side, Papa sprung from the boat.

"Hold tight, Cricket," he said, pulling the line and towing the boat up onto land.

Climbing from the rowboat I found myself looking up at the enormous crags. The trees were also immense, much larger than anything I had seen before.

Suddenly, I realized how small I truly was. I thought of all the stories and tales I had heard about the wilderness. My mind fluttered into images of *'The Big Bad Wolf'*. Before my eyes I saw grizzly bears, cannibals, the ugliest and most gruesome figures ever designed. I was petrified in thought but exhilarated in heart. I wanted to climb up into those dark nooks in the rock and live like that character in *The Hatchet*.

Papa tied the bow line and then came up behind me. His size and strength comforted me.

"So, Cricket, you ready for the hike?"

"Yes, let's do it."

I scrambled wildly in my ascent, using all four of my limbs. Papa with his thick German legs nearly floated up the rocks. I wheezed after each burst of energy. Grime and mud caked my palms. Black soot crawled under my fingernails as I scraped and smeared up the boulders.

Higher and higher we climbed. I could not look down. I knew if I were to look back I would freeze, trapping myself on what felt like sheer cliff. Keeping my eyes locked on Papa's back seat, I continued.

At one point Papa stopped. He perched himself on a log that butted up against stone. The circumference of the protruding rock platform was maybe six feet and, as he waited, Papa cheered me on.

"Come on, scramble, little Cricket. You have it in ya," he yelled.

I dug even harder. All any boy ever wants is to be strong, to live up to the expectations of his male kin. At a young age I knew of this line of strong men in my family. It started with Adolph who first came to America in the 1920's, opening a well-known Butcher Shop in New York City.

Pork was his trade.

Following him were a long line of policemen, fire-fighters, union workers, and many more men of the manly variety. The thought was that our blood needed to be strong, with little emotion involved. Fear and death were not topics for discussion. Like philosophy, all were subjects for the softest of hands.

When I reached Papa, he scooted over to give me some space. Throwing his arm around me he gave me an aggressive hug. My eyes rose. My breath leveled. That was when I noticed the vista - the entire panorama of Indian Lake.

Blue water spread for miles. I wasn't sure where sky ended and earth began. White triangular sails glided across the glistening water. The further the water went towards the center, the darker the lake became.

"Isn't it beautiful, Topher?" asked Papa.

"I have never seen anything like it, Papa."

Growing up in Staten Island, I knew the Bay. I'd been in awe of the giant skyscrapers and the suspension bridges that connected the five boroughs. None of that prepared me for this view.

I looked at Papa and it was at that moment, on that hill, above Indian Lake, that I finally felt the full pride and love he had for me. All the great expectations set by our family; the rite of Jones' passage. The generations of strong men had finally accepted me as one of their own.

Papa rolled himself a cigarette on the hill. It was his secret vice - one he continued to hide from the rest of the family. I watched him closely as he dragged long puffs from the unfiltered

Camel. The smoke rolled from his lips and reached out into the blue void above the lake.

"Papa, you know, my Health Teacher told me that smoking was bad for you. It can even kill," I said with concern.

"You know, Topher. There are a lot of things in life that will kill you. I don't think it will be smoking for me."

A Little Shop

Two cute reflections
   smiling in a toaster.

The mothball-sawdust
   tickles the nostrils
like ragweed.

Monofilament fishing-
   lines suspend the
      1970's from the
   timber frame.

Vintage postcards
   of little girls
in sundresses
   and smiling dolphins.

The whole lot of it
covered
   in that persistent stink
of laundry basket.

Before the High Peaks

Outlying chimneys
crumbs when placed against
      the cribbed
Earth that feigns to be part
of the ciphering sky

Copper lawns
as well as the playing fields
      look parched,
almost burnt

(A *Ghost-Master*) inhabits
the post office

Dogs bark relentlessly
at chewing cows
      from kennels
that can only be drowned
out by puffing tractors

And soon will come the
songbirds and the sound
      of fountains
and summer vacation

An Adirondack Road

"Accept loss forever."
Jack Kerouac

My jeep's yellow gas light flickered on. It wasn't until that moment I realized I hadn't checked the fuel gauge in a long time.
"My luck!"
Fortunately, just a short distance on a service station came into view. It was just a bit past the *Jack Rabbit Hostel*. Turning into the station I pulled up slowly to the pumps. While the vehicle filled I ran inside to grab some oil and transmission fluid. The place was packed. A little café was situated in the one corner, tucked up against the big front glass windows. Men in big shouldered flannels hunched over their coffee. Laughing, their big teeth fell out of sun-bleached baseball caps. All this vocal rumbling was comforting.
My eyes scanned the bright coolers. Grabbing a few miscellaneous items I made way to the counter, smiling at everyone I came across. I don't know why but there is something heartening about the unknown stories of strangers, especially here listening to the locals while waiting in line. It was the way they solicited advice from the cashier. The way their kids played behind the cooler doors. It's a warm feeling. There is no place else on earth quite like it.
"That will be $45.98, Sugar," said the cashier.
"Why, thank you very much," I replied,

handing the women the exact change.

After I had paid and completed my vehicle maintenance I was off again, following the pines and hardwoods further north.

Not thirty minutes on, about midway in on that wild wonderful tract from Placid to Wilmington, I noticed something in the road. When I was all but twenty feet from it, its silhouette solidified. It was an injured doe.

I pulled to a stop on the shoulder of the road. I could clearly see her body in uproar - frantic, desperate hoofs scratching ceaselessly on blacktop. Attempting to crawl, not understanding why her body would not respond, the deer's small triune mammalian brain flaring desperately, sending reptilian signals, with all parts of the body in disagreement, knowing instinctively that her only salvation was in the woods, away from the cars, the houses, this road and this man. She crawled, her once strong hind legs now mere sticks dragging behind. A horrible sight.

I could not watch this play out. I knew I had to do something.

I had been in this predicament before - two years before, in fact. In the jungles of Belize I had come upon an injured kinkajou, a Central American mammal belonging to the raccoon family.

The animal had obviously been attacked by something. I had always been taught to leave and let nature take its course; not to interfere, but to stay on the sideline. I had believed that... once.

I couldn't leave the Kinkajou to its end on the

forest floor. I couldn't leave this doe to the road.

I walked slowly up to the creature that was swimming frantically on the chipping pavement. She looked at me with hazel eyes - eyes describing both pain and dumb animal uncertainty. Although frightened at first, a strange calm quickly fell over her. It might have been the beginning stages of shock that calmed her; however, I saw it differently in those moments.

It was as if she knew me to be an angel of mercy.

The doe stopped all movement and looked at me.

"*Shhh,*" I touched her heaving side. Kneeling down beside her, I allowed my hand to run over her copper coat. Her eyes continued watching me. They not only watched me, they seemed to cut into the very makeup of my being. I saw in her eyes my mother and sister. In that doe I saw the fertility of all life... of all women.

"*I'm so sorry. Shhh, it's okay, good girl,*" I began to cry. "*You're broken,*" I whispered.

I touched her head. Petting the deer I watched as blood poured from her smashed pelvis.

As I felt her about to brace and attempt to stumble off I applied the needed pressure. I snapped her neck with one quick movement. She jolted once and then slumped dead in my lap.

"*I'm so sorry,*" I whispered softly.

I sat there for what felt like an eternity. No cars, trucks, nor bikes passed during those moments of this impromptu wilderness wake. Only the silent deer, the endless sky and me - a witness to another sad moment of nature's ever-losing interaction with civilization.

    Dragging the doe off the road as best I could, I gathered branches and pine needles, creating a natural coffin of sorts. I stood, deeply shaken, my stomach in turbulence. My eyes blurred with tears. Attempting to walk, I felt at once dazed yet I noticed that everything around me focused into a scene of hyper-reality. All the senses sharpened.
    In the jeep I changed my blood-soaked clothes. I cleaned up as best I could, started the truck, and glanced back for one final look.

    I headed out again onto that long Adirondack Road.

10,000 Sugar Shacks

1.

I hear, fire
    whistling in the valley.
10,000 sugar shacks boiling
sap at once
caramelizing the air

2.

Pale electric
    lamps
burning from kitchen
windows,
creating a spectacle
        of grounded
suns sown to the indigo landscape.

3.

Where unfilled space above
    the pasture
captures a distant highway.
Its reverberation making something
    like a whale song.

In My Time
(A Short Experimental Sketch)

After the *'Woody Allen'* film we left the theater. Outside, orange bulbs burned above the wet sidewalk. Tammy and Julia walked ahead. Daniel and I followed.

The women's blue umbrella covered most of their bodies, except for exposed legs that hung *'sous les auspices de'* and entered high heels. Traffic passed and tires 'hushed' by on drenched pavement. We approached the crosswalk.

We had only recently met the O'Brien's. Julia had received an invitation for a "Tycoon" party that was being hosted at the O'Brien's home. The party was a sensation and the four of us had hit it off immediately.

"So it will be oysters and martinis, yes?" asked Tammy.

"That sounds fabulous, Honey," replied Daniel.

We all agreed *"Chez Pierre"* would be the only suitable establishment.

It was a short wait once we arrived and soon enough we were armed with martinis and conversation *(summers in Indian Lake; winters in Lake Placid)*. The drinks were perfect. With Grey Goose Vodka as a base, they had the right amount of olive juice with no Vermouth.

"It's so hard to find a dry dirty martini in this town," complained Julia.

"No vermouth. That's the way I like it - dry and dirty," exclaimed Tammy.

Dish and glass clattered. The restaurant was

a touch crowded although only I seemed to notice that fact.

Julia and Daniel were off in the midst of a grand conversation about Education in America.

The Oyster Trio arrived and we shared it, but for Julia, who had the Crème brûlée.

"*I don't eat creatures,*" Julia snarled.

"*How long have you been a vegetarian?*" Dan inquired.

"*Oh, for about sixteen years now. It all started once when my father brought home a basket of trout from a fishing trip. I asked him why he was cutting off their faces. It was at that point that my father banished meat of any sort from our diet,*'" Julia said, laughing at the tale.

Tammy and I verbally jousted about literature and poetry.

"*Is there a place for poetry in America today?*" Tammy asked.

"I believe it is crucial if we have any hope of remembering the truth behind our modern America," I replied.

"*What do you mean?*" Tammy inquired.

"Well, historians collect the facts about culture and societies, looking at numbers, carrying capacities, big events. The Social Ecologist and Anthropologist, like the poet, instead capture the truth of sociology, the subcultures within and..."

"*That's a hunk of crap!*" interrupted Julia. "*The historian moves through the process of analysis, which involves investigation and description of what actually happened. He's based in variables and in deciphering what happened so that artifacts, art, story can be taught in fact rather than artistic expression.*"

After dinner we went for a drive in the

O'Brien's new sports car. We rounded the corners of Saratoga like LA bandits until, in the light of the sun's rising next day, Julia and I were dropped off at our cottage.

"Are you coming in for coffee?" Julia asked.

The O'Brien's followed us in through the front door.

The rest is history.

Astronomy

I see no angels. There's plenty of night,
and big planes flying through it.

The rafters shake. I can feel its quake.
Through the shingles pressed-up against
my shoulder blades.

Over-yonder, brick stacks spew night-crawlers.
The moon looks speckled. If I hadn't known any
better, I might've confused it with Jupiter.

The whole thing is wrong. It looks battered.
This is not the heaven I knew as a child.

What will I say one day when my children ask
"Daddy, what's a star?"

Let's Return to the Trail
For: Heather

Let's return to the years
we built trail together,
but this time let's break
new turf.

It can be anywhere,
as long as it's a place
without sidewalk.

And when we get there,
I'd ask if we could idle
      for a while.

We could make bitter faces
at one another; eating
beechnut in tall grass.

Finding ourselves
watching a worried
mallard search for
      her groom.

I would love to cry
once more in the fading
crimson daylight, but only
if it was with you.
And only if you promise
never to tell anyone.

Siamese Ponds

"To go in the dark with a light is to know the light. To know the dark, go dark. Go without sight, and find that the dark, too, blooms and sings, and is traveled by dark feet and dark wings."
        Wendell Berry

  It was late August. The thick heavy air and looming thunderheads gave one the feel of early July. We had just hiked four miles and reached the first lean-to. We decided, given the group's pace and ability, that it would be best to set up camp in and around the lean-to. Spanning before this structure was a thirty-five foot steel suspension bridge gliding over a small trickling brook.
  Camp was set up in a matter of minutes. Given all the wildlife signs we had come across during our trek in, we spent some extra time surveying the site for an adequate bear bag spot. The rich wildlife of the Siamese Wilderness Area is well known in the Adirondacks and throughout most of New York State. The bio-diversity is magnificent. Usually mammals are harder to spot in the Northeast, but in the Siamese region the signs and marks of animals can be found around every tree trunk. White-tailed deer. Black bear. Coyote. Bobcat. Beaver. Otter. Mink. The previous summer in this same area, just a few miles down-trail at the ponds, I had heard five different loons screaming in the dusk light...

Only in the Adirondacks...
I watched one of our members priming the whisper-light stove in preparation for the evening dinner.

After a solid evening repast, we moved off to our designated places. The group had various tents strung about. Clint, Lucy, and I shared the one staff tent. It was a three-person Mountain Hardware. Clint had worked at *The Mountaineer* in Keene Valley the previous year and thus had the best of the best when it came to outdoor gear. In the light of our headlamps we studied the map, trying to plan for the following day. While deep in meditation, we heard a strange noise. It sounded as though it was close to the edge of the camp's perimeter.
"*Did you hear that?*" Lucy whispered.
"*Yeah,*" Clint and I replied in one voice.
Again, the same sound. A whimpering almost - a puppy yelping.
"*I think it's a cub,*" Clint thought out loud.
"*A cub, shit,*" I blurted out.
Lucy started breathing heavily. I felt a slight panic. I had never seen bear in the wild before; only those on the Discovery Channel. I knew only the theoretical when it came to bears. (*Years later I would come face to face with a five hundred pound black bear in the Vermont wilderness and would think back to this night.*)
We exited the tent, preparing ourselves to encounter the wild and the hostile. Armed with headlamps, full water bottles, and some multi-

tools, we looked about the camp. We made noise in order to let the bear know we were people and not for eating. We also wanted the bear to know we would stand and fight - the common approach to defensive measures against black bears in North America.

In a few minutes we heard rustling across the stream. There, in the dim light from our campfire and flashlights we saw three sets of blue glowing eyes. It was like looking into the heart of the forest, as if everything within this strange wild place recognized you as alien to its landscape.

"*Holy shit, look,*" Clint muttered. It was a big sow and two cubs, not twenty-five feet away.

"*Hey! Hey! Hey!*" Clint, than Lucy, then I began screaming. We increased our volume and in a flash of shadow and brush all three bears vanished.

With nervous laughter we hugged in the dark forest under the Adirondack stars.

Lying in my sleeping bag, I thought of the bears, of the mountains, of my life beyond Staten Island. I imagined my trip to Belize upcoming in the fall. I thought of the potential of my life as a wild pilgrim, chasing dreams across the untouched places of the world. As my thoughts fell slowly into the quiet abyss of sleep, I was jolted awake by a terrifying sound.

"*Oh, God, I'm going to die!*"

The three of us in our tent were horribly startled by the cry from outside.

With knife in hand, dressed only in his

boxers, Clint slipped quickly out of the tent. I prepared to follow. Lucy grabbed me and pleaded for me to stay.

"*No, no, he needs me,*" I tried to struggle free.

Lucy grabbed my face, "*You can't leave me here.*"

At that moment, reminded of Hollywood adventure films from the 1950's, I thought of kissing her... but didn't.

A moment later Clint reentered the tent, sweating, wet, panting.

"*What happened?*" we demanded.

Clint looked at us in an exhausted state. "*Kevin, Kevin... from Albany...*"

"*Yes, Kevin... what?*"

I expected blood, guts, claws, possibly even death - anything but what Clint reported. "*Kevin had a nightmare.*"

In the black tent, under the giant trees, with thunder murmuring over the hills to the west, we tried to sleep - huddled together, waiting for nature to decide on its meteorological course. We were only guests in this wilderness.

It was only when the sun started to form among the trees, and the first birds of morning awoke in the air, that we slept.

Lunch at Noonmark

Inside strong coffee boiled
and steak sizzling like the branding of steer.
To my surprise the smell of baking overtook
the aroma of grass-fed Angus.

Oak tables felt stable under
the pressure of exhausted bodies.
The place was loud and comfy.
It could almost have been confused with
Thanksgiving.

And even though the waitress
was plain, there was something about
her that kept my attention.

Over the bar is a slate board scripted
in colorful chalk, listing a variety of warm pies;
strawberry rhubarb being my favorite of the
bunch.

George Eve
(Lake George Nights)

It wasn't the bustle
of women that trapped
my heart each summer.
*Though I did enjoy
their passing perfume
on the 'Village.*

In the open I'd watch
the earth's lining.
Its mountains spooning
the purple universe.

Moths and other night time
insects danced around black
lampposts like many of
my awkward friends.

Even with the street lights
on, the view was good
because the stars above did
what stars do best.

James Morgan of Diamond Point

"*Great men, unknown to their generation, have their fame among the great who have preceded them, and all true worldly fame subsides from their high estimate beyond the stars.*"
　　　　　　　　　　　Henry David Thoreau

I've only met a few folk in this world who have truly changed me. The one I speak of today is James Morgan. James is the type of man you would most likely see in a local hardware store, a figure whom you might pass by in your speeding car while trying to escape *Diamond Point,* only to, years later, remember the moment you glanced back into the rearview mirror to a vanishing figure carrying a basketful of vegetables.

If you're lucky enough you might even have purchased one of his small hand-carved smiling black bear trinkets sold at a dozen different Adirondack Gift Shops.

***

I thought it was early morning although I awoke with a strange feeling. It could have been the previous night at the *George Henry.* Or maybe it had something to do with the color of the walls at the Cornerstone B&B. Either way, I dressed and headed out with my complimentary coffee-to-go for a walk.

To be sure, the day had begun without me. It was actually close to noon and the bright July sun was blanketing the eastern world. My shades gave little relief. After several blocks I stepped into *'Marco Polo's Pizzeria'* for air-conditioning and a cold drink. I sat at the counter and was greeted by a husky man in a stained apron.

"*What can I do for you?*" he asked.

"*Can I get a Coke! Oh, and umm... how about a mushroom cheddar slice?*"

I ordered in a tone as non-threatening as possible for someone with a Brooklyn accent visiting the North Country - *something I continuously strive for here in the mountains.* Blue me, quietly staring out the restaurant windows, admiring the trees beyond the town.

The Adirondacks...

My peripheral vision caught the movement of a man passing in front of the restaurant. The bell rang as the patron entered. The man gave a subtle glance towards the owner - the husky, apron-wearing man.

"*Hey, Jim, how are you?*" cackled the owner.

"*Oh, you know, the world's still turning,*" the new customer replied.

His tone was comforting, grandfatherly, but from my telling he was not much past forty. He wore a long dirty blonde ponytail under an old painter's cap, torn-up overalls, solid leather work boots. His hands rested in a prayerful position on the counter. They were farmer's hands, maybe even carpenter's hands.

The man took a deep breath and sighed.

"*Hello there! By God, I didn't even notice anyone else was here,*" he said and approached me with a big toothy smile. "*I'm James Morgan, but folks around these parts call me Jim.*" He extended his hand as he popped onto the stool next to me.

My pizza slices arrived shortly and I shared them with *Mr. Morgan*. I mean *Jim*. We talked about everything. Jim told me all about his life in the north country. We spanned the entire state in a thirty minute conversation. *Keene Valley. The Finger Lakes. Bear Mountain. Chipmunk. Colby. Colgate.* He told me of his daughter who was attending Skidmore College in Saratoga.

I opened up to this stranger, something I was not accustomed to doing much, especially to a backwoods carpenter with a ponytail. I told him about my blues, the struggles I had growing up in Staten Island, the uncertainties I had about life. I discussed my drinking, my issues with commitment. I even went into all of my financial woes. Nothing was secret. From the intensity of our conversation, the owner seemed to fade back into his kitchen.

"I appreciate the difficulty of putting it in words..." Jim started. *"It's all stuff that I know you kind of wear on your sleeve - along with your heart... a good thing, really."*

Jim told me how he had noticed my sad face around town, and, knowing most everyone in town, he recognized that I was most likely a modern-day pilgrim, searching for some luck, searching for something. There weren't many places to go in the east. He told me all eastern roads led to the Adirondacks.

"I was an asshole at your age... relationship-wise... well, a lot of other-wise, too...," he chuckled.

"But you are such a sage. I couldn't imagine you a punk, blue early twenty-something," I replied in protest.

Ignoring my reaction, he continued, *"Listen,*

you have health, youth, and even love... about 90% of all sentient beings would trade that for some debt. Just keep plugging along."

Jim smiled and placed the money on the counter for the food and soda. *"And Topher? Maybe when you find your way back to the Adirondacks..."* He paused. *"After you've figured yourself out... I think maybe you should come on back. The two of you could be good friends."*

"The two of who?" I was puzzled.

"My daughter! You two would get along fine," he suggested as he walked towards the glass door.

September's in my bones

My head's a salamander.
Inside my boots, my feet
carry on like slugs.

I can feel September in my bones.
Golden light hovers
between gathering birch trees.
Sipping on what remains of
      Irene.

North Country for Old Men

The remoteness is backing away.
Tectonic rocks pile
 into coliseum walls.
Common grackles become bossy,
guarding their carrion
 from the roadside.
Already the little diners have become smaller,
while the *Ford* trucks
 have grown to colossal size.
Old coveralls suit heavier in
 collecting snowfall.

 ***

It helps to wear callused hands here
in the winter.

Winter Air

Nine o'clock seemed to follow swiftly from daybreak. We'd been turkey hunting since five am. Our hope was to arrive early so as to place ourselves close to the roosting flock. After finding a spot to park, Clint and I headed up the high road, while his father (Clark) and sister (Libby) headed downtrail towards the river.

For four cold hours Clint and I huddled down on snowpack. Wearing waterproof pants helped but the conduction from the ground pulled every last bit of warmth from our bodies. When light broke Clint pulled a turkey call from his coat pocket. Starting with a soft series of yelps and clucks - Clint slowly increased his volume and aggressiveness, thinking that maybe the gobblers were further away, or perhaps the louder sound would attract them.

I usually mixed up my calling by switching types of calls, helping to confuse the turkeys a bit. If you hunt the same area over and over again the turkeys become aware of the sound and its consequence, *though some people may disagree with the intelligence of these birds.*

After two hours with no success sitting or stalking, I pulled a flask from my inside pocket. Inside the flask were 5 ounces of *Hudson Corn Whiskey*. Leaning against the trunk of a big red oak, we shared the warming liquor. The buzzing sensation of the whiskey brought some red back into our cheeks.

"I don't think we're going to have any luck today, Topher. The woods have been pretty congested all fall. Everything is hunkering down, refusing to move. I know the State's *Land Management Plan* says we have 'plenty of game', but each year my father and I have watched these woods become more and more barren. It's a shame."

"I haven't hunted a whole lot in New York, but I can tell you this is an issue all over the Northeast. I think Federal and State Biologists have their own agenda," I replied.

"I gave up on government a long time ago," he said and then became silent.

We took another swig before standing up to stretch our legs. The hard snow crunched below our boots.

"Well, I guess it's time to head back. You know, I don't think that Dad and Libby will get anything. Most of the game stays up in this warmer pine cover. That lower trail gets all exposed when hardwoods drop their leaves."

"Yeah, maybe, but Clint, remember when Libby bagged all those pheasants? Man, she was the only one who got anything that whole trip."

"Yeah, but she is a friggin' scary shot. She uses that spray and pray method. I swear one day she is going to hurt somebody."

It was then that three consecutive shots rang through the winter air.

Willow Cracked Sidewalk

They come and go with little regard
for things happening in the fin.
They've all packed their wicker baskets
with sunshine from nearby fields.

A clan of mint-topped *Bridge players*
resemble decorated yellow-jackets
plotting amid the swarm of honey bees.

There the red felt tips of sumac
are blooming in the cemetery.
Eastern marble shaped and marooned
on the hillside.

Church doors open and devour
waddling women in Easter hats.
Gothic and chilly, the inside
reminds me of a London train station.

The daylight is warm,
with a lasting October chill.
My penny loafer accidentally scrapes
the willow cracked sidewalk.

Two otters occupy themselves
in the bottle green river.
Their playfulness causing me to miss
that special someone.

At the Potholes

Long time it's been since
    I've propelled
        through the air, on a rope-swing.
A rocky river bottom,
    rocketing towards me
        from eel shaded water.
Leggy children scale
    sandstone cliffs, preparing
        for another go at the fall.
I'm amongst blue jays
    not remembering who I am.
And before I can recall,
    my body breaks the surface of the water
like a stone thrown through a church window.

(A buoyant object anchored in a sea.)

When my lungs burn
    I push from the pebbles
        and harpoon upward.

    This time breaching already broken surf
in carbonation, rumbling in the eddy.

Pharaoh Lake

With a head heavy
   in ancient idiom.
I sat wine drunk
in the open moon.

My copy of
   'Mammal Tracking',
frayed from years
of camp use.

An arid pine-needle
   substrate,
confirms the forester
was correct, this place
had been burnt by wildfire.

Dare I call for
   a hen loon,
without receiving
harsh criticism in front
of all these
winking tree frogs.

Crane Pond Road

"You know, Crane Pond has quite a bit of history to it," said the old man sitting beside me at the campfire.

Sunset was upon us and the stranger knew he needed to be getting home, but something kept him in place.

It could have been my interest in the pond, or maybe perhaps he was just a lonely old coot. For whatever reason, he chose to share his tale with me.

"Well, you see this truck road here is popular with hunters, fishermen, and flatland backpackers like yourself," said the old man pulling at his corn cob pipe and chuckling at my expense.

Above us a thin moon appeared low in the sky. In the distance I could hear a chorus of green frogs banjoing a welcoming twilight.

"Now, the land planning here is rather dubious," he said in an irritated tone. "All these lands are not wilderness...*(cough)* but ya see is only... (*cough*), el-e-elected as such by bureaucratic ink," the man coughed and tweezed between uncertain points.

"You see, son, my friends and I, we've spent our entire lives playing in these parts. Our fathers- fathers all hunted and fished here. We got deer camps all about." The man became more animated, waving his arms in all directions, trying to dictate where all these events and places were situated.

***

Back behind where we now sat was Crane Pond Road. Everywhere the landscape was pleasing to the eye. The topography had gently rolled beneath my leather hiking boots earlier in the day.

The road was situated between a thick understory of vegetation. I had noticed that groves of striped maple buffered the interior of the forest. The white birch trees stood out between the almost purple trunks of white pine, reminding me of rhinoceros's skin.

At one point during my hike a boulder sitting to the right side of the road had caught my eye. Weathered and covered in dead lichen the stone sat in a spot just off the hardened road.

I investigated further by brushing off handfuls of brown pine needles. Words appeared. Faded, almost illegible: 'ADIRONDACK HOMELAND'.

***

"It's definitely a rough road," I said to the man as I fiddled with the logs on the fire.

"You're damn right. Shit, yah! It's rough country, full of rough people and that's how we like it. You see, all these people making decisions about this land. Well, son, they don't live here."

For all accounts he was right. Many of the Park's decisions are made by little men sitting back in big leather chairs in offices above the smoke stacks of Albany, looking out at us from big binoculars, pretending to know what's happening here.

I offered the man some of my water in hopes of relieving his constant cough.

"No, no, I'm fine," he replied under struggling breaths. "So that boulder you mentioned earlier. You came across it up the road?"

"Yes, it was really strange. I..."

"That has a lot to do with what I was just sayin' about this truck road here."

"What do you mean?"

The man looked at me wide-eyed in the glow of the now-smoldering coals. He checked his watch and saw that it was much later than he had expected. In his thoughts he imagined his wife at home annoyed yet again by his lateness. Inside he snickered a little. She must have thought he was out getting drunk in the moonlight... "I am just about to tell you," he barked, coming back to the subject at hand.

"It was back in 1990. You must have been a little tyke back then?"

"Yeah, about six."

"So, it was 1990 and this here road had gotten little attention from anyone. It was decided by those crooks in Albany to close the road. It seemed that some environmental-god-righteous folks, you know, those pinheaded pencil dicks that would piss their pants if they ever came across a bear - " *I laughed.* "Well those same pencil dicks weren't going to enforce anything..."

"So what happened?"

"When the road continued to get used, a group of flatlanders showed up and tented right in the middle of the goddamn road." The old man laughed in amazement past a missing tooth which I hadn't noticed until just that moment. He slapped his brown reinforced work pants that sent sawdust out from below his slapping pats.

"The sheriff showed up at the request of a few locals and, well, one of them protesting boys got what he deserved." The man punched his right fist into his left palm and yell "Whaaap!"

It startled me in the dark.

Later I found an old news article about the "Battle of Crane Pond Road". It had been quite a big deal, and, unfortunately, had ended with a law enforcement officer losing his job because of the confrontation.

"So what happened next?"

"The state needed to save face so they placed some boulders in the road to try and stop access by truck."

I leaned over and added another log to the dying fire, blew on the smoldering ashes, blazing the newly dried log.

He continued. "A masked group removed the boulders in the night and vowed to keep the road open."

"Did they ever figure out who they were?" I asked.

"Nope. They are good folk, I vow. *Adirondack Homeland* is a statement. It don't only count for roads. It's the entire park. All of these places. All of our homes."

"So, come on, you are telling me you don't know who moved the boulders?" I asked again while fiddling with a stick in the fire.

"They're like ghosts. Came in. Did what they

needed to do without hurting anyone."

The moon now had a thicker crescent to it. Everything around us seemed still and content in the dark. The croaks of bullfrogs announced that night was here and that it was time for this old local to be heading home.

"Good talkin' to ya," said the old man standing from his stump. "I share this with you because you seem to have a good head on your shoulders. You remind me of my grandson. He's a good educated man like you. I hope you do something good with this knowledge."

I promised him in little words that I would.

When he walked off into the trees I heard shortly the echoing growl of a truck engine. The ground shook and suddenly it was as if daylight appeared via truck headlights. I watched the old heap turn about and in a quick flash from a tail light made out a large bumper sticker which read "Adirondack Homeland ".

Avalanche Garden

It's a rigid coil which carries the blue
morning over the ice cover.

Warmth taking the shape of chickadees
roughhousing in the hollow.

My snowshoes are treading heavily.
I envision monstrous Pike
slumbering in the deep.

The whole icy place noticing an intrusion,
of soft bodies at the bottom of
this ancient corridor.

It's evident that all the peregrine falcons
have been chased from their
granite homes by a bitter cold.

On either side wide slides threaten
to vomit a world of snow upon us.

Fire in the Sky

The night sky weeping,
children sleeping.
Everyone ignoring lightning
fire behind the mountain.
Fleeting stars bring
no trouble to the cabin.
On the lake portly tadpoles
jump like fierce piranha.
Quickening the grief of a
green-eyed pier.
Watching for the coming
Kingfisher.

North Country Auger

It wasn't until crossing the covered bridge that day began to open over the outlying hills of town. On either side of the lazy street the snow banks had crystallized from last night's freeze; an entire world glimmering in the early light.

***

The plastic sled scraped the gritty snow that roofed the icy pond. The absolute openness of the pond was breathtaking. Granite cliffs and blue ice flows attempted to hide behind the distant homes and pines, but their sheer size did not allow it.

Father Monroe and I passed three shanties before we arrived at the "perfect" spot.

"This looks like it, son," yelled the priest from beneath his buff.

A wind came about, frigid and severe. Any exposed skin felt like it was becoming frostbitten. Pulling a thermometer from his pocket, Father Monroe showed me a reading of nine below zero.

"This is where you find the *real* men," the priest said cheerfully.

Unlike the other anglers on the lake, we had no shanty. As a substitute we had brought with us two empty sheetrock buckets to sit on.

Other items in the sled were a big dull blue auger, a light fishing rod with small, brightly colored jigs, and our bait which included wax worms and fat heads.

"Topher, why don't you pull out that auger and give it a whirl," instructed Father Monroe.

It seemed simple enough. Using one hand to stick the blade end down and grasp the button handle, while placing my other hand on the middle of the rod, I began to turn the instrument just as you would a bit and brace. The only difference was that there was not a bit, so the fanning blades would have to cut down into the ice, catch, and then continue with a downward motion.

Father Monroe said the ice was thick today. "A whole seven inches..." which in my mind wasn't comforting, but ice that was potentially thick enough to drive a car upon. Still, I didn't think that particular thought sounded like a good idea.

(I think my fear of falling through the ice of a frozen lake came from growing up in the city where no one ever walked on an ice-covered lake. All of our urban experience of this came from the movies.)

Daydreaming about all the tales I had ever heard about winter lakes in the Adirondacks, I was suddenly surprised when the tip of my auger finally cut through and my entire body jolted with the cracking hard ice.

"Don't lose that auger. I've had it for ten years and don't plan on buying another one," said Father Monroe.

The priest taught me all about setting up and continuously ladling the hole. This remedial task made sure that the ice did not freeze up your fishing portal.

Once everything was prepared Father Monroe and I sat in the vastness of the cold world and awaited our submerged prey.

In the entirety of it, there was a howling silence. It was cold, god-awful cold, but I dared not complain. I knew that to Father Monroe this was life. This was God.

My body eventually became so bitten by the wind that I needed to stand.

"That's right to get the blood moving back inside ya," said the clergyman who was also looking a bit frost-nipped himself. Reaching into his bag the father pulled out some red wine and bread. "Now, I know you haven't been baptized a Catholic, but I'm moved by the Holy Spirit, or maybe by this awful cold, to give you a little of the Lord's mercy."

Father Monroe handed me the wine. I slugged back on it and let its warm content hit my stomach hard. The fire of the spirits moved out into my limbs. Once again I felt whole as my blood circulation seemed to be warming my body. The priest too took a swig of the cherished Blood of the Savior.

***

Six subzero hours passed. The ladle scoops turned like hour hands in the black hole of the pond.

I jigged and jigged and when I thought the muscles in my hand couldn't jig anymore, I felt a slight tug at the line. The sudden change in rhythm brought both Father Monroe and me back into the moment.

"You have something," he whispered.

I slowly stood from my bucket. Placing my feet and shoulder squarely, I prepared for the battle.

Intentionally jerking hard, I lodged the hook into the mouth of whatever it was that swam below. The fish felt the inflicted danger and began to race off into the icy abyss, but to no avail. I had stuck him deep.

Around the hole I spun, desperately attempting to wrap the line around my rod. It was not a mechanical reel so I had no technical advantage besides my limbs. I then dropped to my knees, forgetting about the rod-stick. Using my mitten-bound hands I pulled and pulled at the line. It hurt, but the material over my hands gave some relief. I could feel Father Monroe hovering nervously above me, like some weird guardian angel of the *Sports Afield* variety. I ignored his peering shadow.

I could see a silhouette circling from beneath the hole. A glimpse of metal and scale shined from the water. It looked almost reptilian, and then the six inch diameter hole filled with teeth and gills. Long and splendid, the face of a giant pike emerged through the opening and into the blue.

Father Monroe pulled out a pair of vise grips and snagged the mouth. Biting into the metal pliers the fish would not give. Behind its big head followed three feet of slender serpentine body.

It was quite a big feat on this my first day of ice fishing. Not quite the adventure I had expected, but memorable nonetheless.

A Portrait As It Should Be...

The radio admits schools *are* closed.
And that's when the runny nose children begin chasing the hillside with wooden sleds.
They do not envy those noodling in the cypress swamps in sunburned Georgia.

***

In century old rocking chairs sitting by warm cast iron, *Depression Era* grandmas enjoy knitting mittens for their squirrelly brood of hot chocolate addicts in pearl ice-skates.

Father's muck boots track the backyard onto the porch and into the oak-floored kitchen.
Lucky for us wooly carpets have lost favor, but occasionally you might find a *'Welcome'* mat in a mudroom accompanying many mothball overcoats.

On the outbuildings, clean icicles dangle like wind chimes in the blue morns of turkey season. The nearest wild flock is just as chilly as Dad's privileged hens, so they sit in feathered roosts awaiting Spring.

***

I don't always recognize the wood this time of year,
but this stand of hunched evergreens are always reassuring.

***

The grocery shops I spoke of have given way to *Co-ops*.
Not much has changed, the smiles are still warm and
It's funny to think that Kale is a new trend, when it's been there with its ruffled leaves all along.

***

I wasn't born a cold earth wanderer, though my father-in-law, would like
to think so.
And everyone in the state trusts his opinion.
So, I guess I too will agree with his sentiment.

Their jade needles, along with my girlfriend
always inspire me not to write awful poetry.

Edwin Arlington Robinson is a good hero and
worth reading.
So many of the aged dogs have vanished in the
sawdust of good ole' New England Libraries
You could probably blame Congress for cutting
budgets and trees
for the purpose of constructing new highways.

***

I continually practice growing beards in the snow
and by the time they're finally refined, the black
flies are hatching and it's too warm to be grizzly.

***

That's what is welcoming about warming our cars
and trucks before leaving for work each morning.
Even when I have to shovel my way to the driver's
side door and pour what's left of my hot coffee on
the handle in order to defrost the lock.

That's what is welcoming about knowing everyone
standing in the grocery line.
Recommending you to put back the celeriac
because
They've had a successful harvest and would love to
share.

That's what's comforting about being on the school
board and participating in every *Town Planning
Meeting.*

The Orchard
RIP: Cody B.

Witnessing fallen leaves gather
on the grass reminds me of
a dead friend.
It's not hard to die, but it's awful
to be left behind.
Valor counts for nothing
in the cold ground.
His memories wilting
in the branch buds.

I dreamt of his body in turbulence.
And today, I witnessed the fall
of *God* in the orchard.
I've learned all beings
are subjects of hell.
After that there was nothing left,
but blind faith
and even that faded.

Spiders and the Hermit's Homestead
For: Sean T.

Lonely house spiders are tormented
by schools of airborne insects outside
the homestead.
Generations of these arachnids have called
these ceiling corners home.
Harvesting all the biting flies that've plagued
the farm barn since its naming all
those wood milling years ago.

Gothic's North Face

"There are only three sports: bullfighting, motor racing, and mountaineering; all the rest are merely games."
  Ernest Hemingway

Sheer ice face. Brutal wind. Confidence draining from my body. My crampon's contact with the ice tenuous. Perspiration pouring from my brow, gathering inside my goggles, the fog over my eyes adding yet another layer to this predicament.

I pressed my body against the mixed ice hoping the angle would keep me on the face. Despair just a breath away. I wanted to cry. I was alone. To die here was a very real possibility.

Fifty meters above me stood Hunter on belay.

I looked down.

Why did I do that? What was I thinking?

White snow, bluish ice and distant trees anchored the world below. Hell itself (a frozen version) seemed to be teasing me, calling to me in these high peak winds.

"Come-on, Topher. I've got you. Just like before. Remember... easy deliberate moves." Hunter's voice above me.

Another gusty wind pulled at me. Leaning into my ice tools and grinding my teeth, I held hard against the mountain. I needed to stay on my points.

The ice was thin. I could feel rock under my

picks just below the surface. The rope was taut, but I had no faith in the belay. Hunter was strong, but he would not be able to hold my full fall off his hip belay. If I fell my total force would either rip Hunter from the wall, or pull the ropes through his mitts.

My only way out... *was up*.

We couldn't manage a rappel from this point. There was no turning back.

We had opted for the least traveled of the three ice climb routes up Gothic's north face. Once you reach the base of the mountain you must traverse from east to west. This route is more technically demanding than the others. On the ascent of the face you need to stay to the right of the large rock outcropping that dominates the western side of the face. Once you top out it's a short hike to the summit.

On our route to our current point we had come across a variety of snowpack. We were there early enough in the year so that avalanche was not a big concern, but as a precautionary measure we had conducted a snow pit analysis at the start of the climb. Conditions had been safe.

After a quick bite of cheese and a *Snickers*, we had started out.

Now I'm hanging here, regretting it all. I should have stayed home. Should have avoided this whole damn game of risk...

Hunter had taken the lead up the heavy base. Being the more experienced climber, Hunter had planned to lead the entire way. He was confident in my belay and that he would be able to work me through the extreme crux moves towards the end of the climb.

It had started off easy. *Too easy.* The first bit of the climb reminded me of a bunny-slope. We had walked up most of this section without hooking into any protection. *Real smart ass.*

As the terrain steepened and the snow iced over, we stopped and placed on more gear. Crampons were strapped over our plastic boots. A climbing rope was pulled out and thrown and we tied ourselves in to one another. We only welded one ice tool for the start. The safety measure here was that if one of us fell and began to slide off the face, one or both climbers could perform a self arrest. *A self arrest is a maneuver in which a climber who has fallen and is sliding down a snow or ice slope arrests (stops) the slide by himself or herself without recourse to a rope or other belay system.*

To ensure safety for some of the sketchier sections during the first half of the climb, Hunter had positioned snow pickets. The pickets were anchored deep into the snow and the rope then clipped into the snow anchor.

Most of the first half of this section was climbed in a mixture of tree and rock cover. It hadn't felt like mountaineering at this stage, except for the gear and clothing we had on.

So far, so good, everything went according to plan. Hunter and I felt good. Cocky bullshit on our part...

Because we had moved swiftly from our camp in the early morning and began climbing before daybreak, we planned to be off the summit by late afternoon. *Good idea to get down from the summit before 3:00 pm. This practice is most important out west or on bigger mountains, but as a good practice Hunter and I chose to stick to this timetable.*

Would never have imagined a year ago that I would be on this epic climb. First climb had been on Cones Point in Vermont. Hunter and I'd attempted to circumnavigate the flow and belay from a tree anchor. That silly little slide back then we viewed as epic. Man, if only I could see what climbing really would become one day.

Hunter and I ate lunch. The food warmed us. We proceeded on. Fifteen minutes in from this point the trees dissolved into background designs. *Suddenly, we were the only standing objects on a big freaking face of white.* The boulders shrank and eventually vanished completely until there was nothing but hard pack snow and patches of ice. Here, as we traversed the face, the angle of the world turned. With ice tools in hand, scrambling up snow at a 40 degree angle, this same angle then abruptly began to veer to one of over 45 degrees.

At this point I stayed back and belayed Hunter every forty of so meters. When Hunter either came to a comfortable spot or we ran out of rope, I would follow. We did this a dozen times until we came to the large rock.

The large rock was where we took our time prepping ourselves for the crux. The last pitch of the climb was 50 meters of exposed, ugly ice. It was a place where someone had once fallen and continued to roll, gaining momentum all the time, until his broken body had come to a stop at the gully floor.

In my head I played through the spinning hell that would bring a human back 1,000 feet to where we had begun our climb.

"Goddamn awful," I thought to myself, feeling sick from this image that was playing over and over again in my head.

That is what has stopped me. That is why I am now standing here 900 feet off the earth almost crying. I try to move. I attempt again and again to pull one of my tools and swing the next placement, but I can't.

"Topher, I see you. I will not let you fall. All you need to do is pull and swing your tool above you. It will hold. I promise."

I take Hunter's advice and pull my right tool off the wall. Drawing back so that my right elbow meets the side of my face, I whip the tool above my head. I flick my wrist at the last possible second to insert the perfect tool placement. It is sticking.

"Yeow," screams Hunter, over the wind.

This gives me a bit more courage. My heart still remains lodged in my throat.

I swing with my left tool just as I had done before. The form is perfect, but on impact the ice dinner plates. My body jolts down into my crampons. I think I am going to fall, but my legs hold right. *Jesus, God!*

"Shit, Shit, Shit, Shit, SSShhitt…"

"It's alright! You are still here, you motherfucker. Don't you try to bring me back down there! It took me forever to get up here."

I close my eyes and place my helmet against the ice. I pray. I pray the way I had prayed with my mother as a child. I pray to a God I haven't prayed to in years. I call out to a God that I blamed for taking my Grandfather all those years ago. I am at his unknown mercy.

"Ok, Topher. Let's try this again."

I remember how scared I had been many times before. How each and every time I thought I would die. So many times in the past I had thought I wouldn't be able to go on… but had. Time after time experiencing the loss of lovers or a loved one, but I am still here. It isn't my time. I know that now.

I climb on.

Tragedy in the Kingdom

The sow sits alone in the balsam dark.
Her cub chased away.
Most likely killed by a pack of snarling
dogs and anxious men.
Wielding cruel guns in an otherwise
peaceful kingdom.

This first year mother grunts
with a reaching upturned lip *(mourning)*...
The scent of her yearling dissolves
in the stirring forest.

The acorn will not please her,
nor the ripened blackberries weighty
on the prickly green.
For a little while anyway, everything
will be at a loss.

About the Author

Born in Brooklyn, New York, Christopher Ricker became familiar with the natural beauty of the Adirondack Park during a four year seasonal journey throughout the region. During his time there he kept journals and raw excerpts which eventually became the basis for *"Lunch at Noonmark"*.

Currently, Chris resides with his girlfriend (*Heather*) in northern Vermont, where he works as a Conservation Program Coordinator and writer.

Other works by Christopher Ricker include:

"Carpenter's Daughter" Ra Press 2011

"Road Poets: On the Road with the Burlington Neo-Beats" Ra Press 2011.

"Nightjar Lyrics" and *"Genesis of Empire"* Thread Magazine, Issue# 3 2011.

"Midnight Highway" Beatdom Magazine, Issue # 9 2010.

"Poetry Blight" Vantage Point, UVM Literary Magazine 2012.